The Spark Files

Book Six

Dark Forces

Illustrated by Philip Reeve

ff

faber and faber

First published in 1999
by Faber and Faber Limited
3 Queen Square London WC1N 3AU

Printed in Italy

Cover design: Shireen Nathoo

A CIP record for this book
is available from the British Library

ISBN 0-571-19741-8

J91,783
£3·99

The Spark Files

Terry Deary trained as an actor before turning to writing full-time. He has many successful fiction and non-fiction children's books to his name, and is rarely out of the best-seller charts.

Barbara Allen trained and worked as a teacher and is now a full-time researcher for the Open University.

To Ben Goakes TD

Be a safe Scientist

Dark Forces

FILE 1

NAME: Simon Spark
(that's me!)

DESCRIPTION: Everyone
calls me Simple Simon. I think
that's cos I'm so clever. To a
genius like me even the hardest
task is 'simple'.

NOTES: Simple Simon is my name
I treat danger like a game!
Tigers take one look and run
Because I fight them just for
fun...

(... so long as they're stuffed
toy tigers, sister Susie says)

FILE 2

NAME: Susie Spark
(my sister)

DESCRIPTION: Susie would be all right if she wasn't so fussy and tidy. She once told me that the cart always comes before the horse because it says so in her dictionary.

NOTES:

Sister Susie, tidy lass,
Sparkles like a looking glass,
Her school socks they have
no holes,
they're even white beneath
the soles!

(...unlike mine which are as black
as puddings, Sister Susie says!)

FILE 3

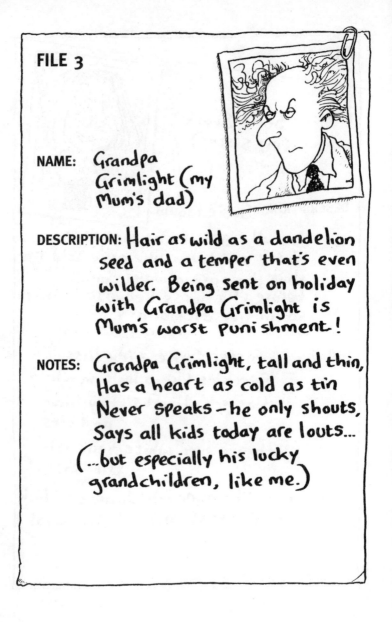

NAME: Grandpa Grimlight (my Mum's dad)

DESCRIPTION: Hair as wild as a dandelion seed and a temper that's even wilder. Being sent on holiday with Grandpa Grimlight is Mum's worst punishment!

NOTES: Grandpa Grimlight, tall and thin,
Has a heart as cold as tin
Never speaks - he only shouts,
Says all kids today are louts...
(...but especially his lucky grandchildren, like me.)

FILE 4

NAME: Motion Man
(a man of
mystery)

DESCRIPTION: This man bought 'Sunshine Funshine Park' on the seafront and turned it into 'Nightmare Park'! They say some people have gone in there and never been seen again!

NOTES: Motion Man, a proper horror!
Say goodbye to your tomorrows
If you meet him in the dark
Of his fairground- Nightmare
Park!
(...though I'm not scared of him, you understand. Well, not much.)

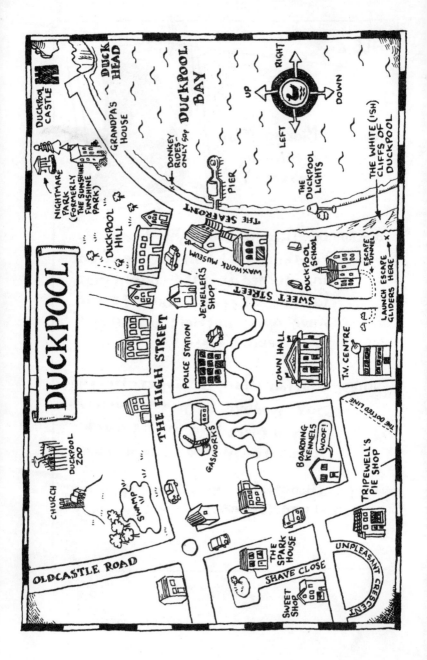

Chapter 1

I'll never forget the news that morning if I live to the age of ten... and I was eleven last birthday!

I was shocked, stunned... and very hungry because Boozle the dog ate my cornflakes while we listened to the morning news on the radio.

...AND POLICE ARE OFFERING A £10,000 REWARD FOR THE ARREST OF THE RUBY ROBBERS WHO WERE LAST SEEN IN OLDCASTLE.

AND NOW HERE IS THE LATEST NEWS FROM DUCKPOOL WHERE THE MOTION MAN HAS STRUCK YET AGAIN! TODAY'S TERRIBLE TOLL STANDS IN DOUBLE FIGURES. YES, TEN CHILDREN HAVE NOW GONE MISSING IN A WEEK. ALL WERE PUPILS AT DUCKPOOL PRIMARY WHERE PANICKING PARENTS ARE PETRIFIED AND POOR PUPILS ARE PRAYING FOR PITY AND FOR PATRICK PEASBODY AND GLORIA GARGLE. OUR REPORTER AT THE SCENE, IVOR STOREY, SENDS US THIS UPDATE. COME IN IVOR!

HI THERE FOLKS! NEVER IN THE HISTORY OF DUCKPOOL HAVE KIDS BEEN SNAPPED OFF THE STREETS SO MYSTERIOUSLY. IN FACT YOU COULD SAY THEY'VE BEEN KID-SNAPPED! HO! HO! KIDNAPPED, KID-SNAPPED, GEDDIT? ANYWAY, I HAVE WITH ME CEDRIC CRUMP, CARETAKER AT DUCKPOOL PRIMARY WHO WOULD HAVE BEEN A WITNESS TO THE LATEST SNATCH IF HE'D SEEN IT! TELL ME, CED, JUST WHAT DID YOU SEE?

EMPTY CRISP PACKETS IN MY YARD LAST NIGHT AT 4 O'CLOCK! THAT SCRUFFY PATRICK PEASBODY USED TO DROP THEM EVERYWHERE. I FOLLOWED THE TRAIL TO GIVE HIM A PIECE OF MY MIND, BUT WHEN I GOT TO THE DESERTED OLD FAIRGROUND THE TRAIL STOPPED. THE LAST PAPER I FOUND WAS A NOTE. IT SAID, "I'VE GOT HIM! SIGNED, THE MOTION MAN!" NEXT THING I KNOW THE POLICE ANNOUNCE SCRUFFY LITTLE PATRICK'S FAILED TO RETURN HOME FROM SCHOOL. EXCITING, ISN'T IT?

BUURP!

8

Gran clutched her throat in horror and switched off the radio... with her other hand. 'You could be next!' she told us kids.

Susie, Sam and Sally turned pale as the milk on my cornflakes. I turned to finish them and found an empty plate! Boozle the dog licked his chops. Baby Spark giggled and gurgled.

'We can't go to school!' I said happily. 'Too dangerous!'

'You're right,' Gran said. 'Duckpool is dangerous. That's why your mum and dad and me have decided to send you all away till the Motion Man is caught!'

'Great!' I cried. 'Where are we going?'

'I'm taking Sally and Sam with me to Magic Mouse Land in Florida,' Gran said. Sally and Sam whooped with joy and ran upstairs to pack.

'Yeah?' I said eagerly. 'Where are Susie and I going then?'

'You twins are going to stay with your Grandpa Grimlight, just up the coast,' Gran said.

My heart sank. My jaw dropped. I'd have thrown up if I'd had any breakfast. 'That's not fair!'

'Yes it is,' Gran said. 'It's right next to the fair, in fact.'

'An empty, disused fair,' I said. 'No fun at all. And Grandpa Grimlight... he's like something out of the Chamber of Horrors!'

'And his house is not the cleanest I've ever come across,' Susie sniffed. 'But I'm sure Simon and I can help him tidy up!'

Tidy up! Me! Tidy up! 'Thank you, Boozle, for stealing my breakfast' I muttered. 'If I'd *had* a mouthful of cornflakes I'd have choked.'

'No!' Gran said. 'You'll have no time for tidying. Your grandpa Grimlight is going to take over your education while you're away from school.'

'Grandpa Grimlight? Take over our education?' Susie blinked.

'Aye,' Gran chuckled. 'He were a bus driver you know!'

Susie nodded wisely. 'Then he'll be able to help with our science homework. We're studying *Forces and Motion* this term.'

'Oh, aye?' Gran said. 'Your grandda Spark was in the forces during the war!'

'No, Gran,' Susie said patiently. '*Forces*... like gravity!'

She picked up a piece of toast from the table, and let it fall onto the carpet. There was a scuffle and a squeal as baby Spark and Boozle the dog fought over it then the wounded dog crawled off into a corner. 'Now,' Susie said. 'Why did that toast fall to the floor?'

'Because you dropped it,' I said.

'No, Simple Simon,' Susie sighed. 'I mean, why did it fall to the *floor*? Why didn't it fly to the *ceiling* or out of the *window*?'

She sounded just like Miss Trout, our teacher. Simon walked in with a video camera he was taking on holiday to Magic Mouse Land so I caught Susie's act and you can see what I mean...

When I tried the experiment the dog snatched the ball and ran off with it before it hit the floor. So I gave up. Susie and I went upstairs to pack our bags, ready to stay with Grandpa Grimlight.

'Hang on, Susie,' I said. 'You said *all* objects are attracted to one another. But *I'm* not attracted to *you*.'

'Yes you are,' she said smugly as she folded her carefully ironed handkerchiefs while I stuffed a tissue in my pocket. 'But you are attracted towards me with just one billionth of your body weight!'

I shuddered. It still sounded too much to me.

'So how come gravity doesn't pull us all the way to the centre of the earth?' I asked.

She placed her pencil case, ruler, lap-top computer and school books in a zip compartment of her bag. (I accidentally forgot to pack my school books. I'd probably remember them when it was too late to go back for them.) 'In 1684 Isaac Newton said that *Every action has an equal and opposite reaction.*

'Aw, what does that mean, Susie?' I groaned.

'It means that your feet are pushing down on the ground because of gravity. But the ground is pushing back exactly the same amount!'

'Is it?' I looked down but I couldn't see it pushing.

'It is,' Susie said. 'If it pushed back *less* you'd sink into it. If it pushed back *more* you'd fly up into the air!' she explained.

I looked at the floor and shuddered. I'd never trust it again. I tried jumping around, hoping I'd catch it out, but every time I landed it pushed back with equal force. I hated to admit it, but Susie was right! Gran called from downstairs, 'If you don't stop thumping on the floor I'll come up there and thump your ear, Simon Spark!'

'It'll hurt your hand an equal and opposite amount to what it hurts my ear!' I called back.

'Want to bet?' she growled.

'No, Gran,' I said.

'So get your bags down here now and let's get going before the Motion Man mangles you!'

I got going!

Chapter 2

Grandpa Grimlight's house was a long walk but Gran strode off and we had to follow or be left to the mercy of the spooky streets. We passed the gas-works, we passed the bus station and then we passed a man and a woman wearing one pair of tights over their two heads.

'Practising for the Olympic Games,' Gran said.

'What games is that?' Susie asked.

'You've heard of the three-legged race? Well that's the one-headed Race!'

The curious couple stumbled past, bounced off a telephone box and scattered little red beads into the gutter and then climbed into a ruby-red car. They drove off down the centre of the road and sent cyclists and cats scattering for the safety of the trees. We walked on past the old fairground and arrived at a house next door to it.

Grandpa Grimlight's house stood in its own grounds.

Probably because no other house would be seen standing next to it.

The garden was overgrown with enough poison ivy, nettles and thistles to hide a herd of man-eating rats. 'You can run the lawnmower over that on Sunday,' Susie said.

'You couldn't run a *tank* over that lot!' I told her.

The house was tall and narrow, five storeys high if you counted the basement and the strange little tower at the top. Grandpa Grimlight probably added that so he could see over the top of the weeds. It was cheaper to add a tower than to cut the grass. The big black door had a greeny-brass knocker and Gran dropped it with a boom like doom.

The door swung open quickly as if he'd watched us coming up the path through the jungle and was waiting. 'What do *you* want?' the old man shouted. He wore a coat as white as his hair... which was a sort of dirty grey.

Gran folded her arms. 'Good afternoon Gordon. These are your grandchildren, Simon and Susie.'

His face was thin as a weasel's and his nose as bent as Captain Hook's false hand. 'Which is which?'

Gran stayed calm but her handbag swung by her side with some menace. Gran's handbag was feared by Boy Scouts from Duckpool to Dongsheng ever since one of them tried to help her across the road. 'You should remember, Gordon,' she said quietly. 'There are three things happen when you get old. The first is that you start to lose your memory.'

'What are the other two?' he demanded.

'I don't know. I've forgotten,' Gran said with a sweet smile. 'They'll be no trouble. They've got school work to keep them busy and I said you'd help with your vast knowledge of buses.'

'I've asked a man from the council to come and cut them down!' Grandpa Grimlight cried.

'I said *buses*, not *bushes,* you deaf old fool!' Gran snapped.

She turned to us. 'Be good,' she said.

Susie smiled, as sweet as a sugared mouse and twice as pink. 'Of course, Gran.'

I noticed the swinging handbag. 'Yeah. All right,' I grumbled.

Then she abandoned us to live with this white-crested parrot of a man. 'Come in!' he ordered and we followed him into the gloom of the dark-panelled hallway. Spiders the size of ten-pence pieces swung from the chandeliers, landed on the webbed walls and coughed as the dust rose from the threads. A rusting suit of armour stared at us through black slits in his helmet and his sword hung in the air, only held up by the cobwebs, I'll swear.

He led the way to the stairs. 'Find a couple of rooms and make yourselves at home!' he shouted. Then he pointed towards an open door at the end of the corridor. 'But keep out of *there*!' he warned.

A green light shone from the room and I walked towards it. 'What's in here then, Grandpa?'

'My workshop with my experiments!' he cried. He hurried towards me but he was too late. I was inside the green-lit room.

A tangle of wires and pipes and glass tubes hung from the ceiling. Bottles of strange, sharp-smelling, bright-coloured liquids bubbled and plopped in bottles and a stuffed wildcat snarled from on top of a cupboard.

'Wow!' I said.

Underneath the stuffed cat was a newspaper cutting with a picture of it in Grandpa Grimlight's arms.

I read it...

Duckpool Daily

Still only 6 pence

LAST GASP OF LAST CAT!

Last night bus driver Gordon Grimlight, 55, found the lair of Britain's last blue-toed wild cat... and gassed it! The cat had its home at the Oldcastle Bus Terminus. When Gordon parked there the fumes from the exhaust of the bus poisoned the rare creature.

Gordon, who has been a bus driver for 35 years, swore, "I am going to give up driving after this tragedy. I plan to devote my life to inventing a bus that doesn't pollute and poison the air! The Powerless Bus!"

Relatives of the cat were not informed of the death because it doesn't have any relatives because it was the last blue-toed wild cat... ever.

'You don't ought to be in my inventing room!' boomed Grandpa Grimlight.

'Don't be silly, Grandpa,' Susie said. 'It needs a good tidy up!'

'No it doesn't. Don't you touch *nothing*!'

I stepped forward quickly. 'What Grandpa Grimlight *needs* is some *help* with his *inventions*!' I said. 'How far have you got, Grandpa?' I asked.

'What? You mean you're *interested*?'

'Yes. We probably inherited our interest in science from you, Grandpa. It's in the blood. Tell us how far you've got!'

The old man looked quite pleased. Susie still sniffed at all the dust but saw another Spark Family adventure in this old house. Grandpa Grimlight took out a sheet of paper and pushed it towards us a little shyly. It was the instructions for making a vehicle...

The Grimlight Anti-Gravity Generator

You need:

1. A tin can with both ends cut out.

2. A ball of modelling clay.

3. A pencil.

4. Two hardback books.

GRAVITY

MORE GRAVITY

What you do:

1. Place one end of one book on the end of the other book to make a ramp.

MORE GRAVITY

GRAVITY

2. Stick the clay ball inside the can halfway between the ends.

3. Use the pencil to mark the outside of the can where the clay ball is positioned.

4. Put the can on the ramp with the pencil mark on the uphill side. Watch it roll up the hill against gravity!

It took us five minutes to set up the experiment. But it worked – try it for yourself! Grandpa Grimlight really had something there.

Susie wandered over to the window and rubbed a clean spot in the grime then peered out. It was late afternoon and growing dark out there. 'Grandpa Grimlight,' Susie said softly, 'is that old fairground next door still open?'

'No, not for years.'

'So why are some of the rides moving?' she asked.

I looked over her shoulder. Sure enough the deserted roundabouts were turning, swings were swinging and the rollercoaster was rolling. I felt a cold slug of fear crawl down my back... or it could have been one of the tenpence-sized spiders slipping down my shirt. Whatever it was, it gave me the creeps. In fact I had THE *CREEPS*!

Cool, innit! Spooky!

781, 783

Chapter 3

'Maybe we should investigate!' I said.

  'Maybe we should find the kitchen, have tea, do our homework and then go and investigate,' Susie said.

Grandpa Grimlight had a curious light in his eyes. Sort of... grim. 'I've always *wanted* to have a look around that place. All the forces and movements at work in there. I could learn a *lot*.'

'When we came past the front of the fair there were signs on the rusty old fences warning people to keep out,' Susie sniffed as she passed me a brush to sweep the kitchen while she dusted off a loaf of bread and polished some teabags. (I'll *swear* that's what she was doing! You've never met *anyone* as fussy!)

'Who owns the fair, Grandpa Grimlight?'

'An old schoolmate of mine, I think. His name is Ebenezer Rugg – it's been sixty years – but he was brilliant at making string puppets and putting on shows. I do remember we called him the Puppeteer!'

'Puppy tear?' I asked. 'Why was the puppy crying?'

Susie raised one eyebrow and said spitefully, 'Simon, if you had twice the brains you'd be a half-wit. Now open one of those tins of beans!'

The beans stood on the table a couple of inches apart. A candle was balanced on pins between them. 'What's this, Grandpa Grimlight?' I asked.

'One of my experiments,' he answered. 'It's another look at gravity. You see how the candles are perfectly balanced?' he asked. 'That's because I've found their *centre* of gravity.'

'So what?'

'So... I can make a see-saw that moves without any force. A Powerless See-saw – one step on the road to a Powerless *Bus*. Look, I'll show you,' he offered.

As he explained I drew the experiment on a piece of paper from Susie's exercise book because it could get me some marks with Miss Trout when we got back to school. Here's the paper...

CANDLE SEE-SAW
A brilliant invention by Simon Spark.

You need: A metal tray, two cans the same height, two thin nails or pins, a long candle

What you do:

1. Scrape some wax from the flat end of the candle so that you can light the wick at both ends.

2. Measure the candle to find the middle and push a nail in each side.

3. Rest the nails on the cans to make a see saw.

4. Place the see-saw on the tray, check that it balances. Light both ends.

> **What happens:** The candle drips wax off one end and then off the other so the candle starts to see-saw all by itself as the centre of gravity changes. Magic!

'Brilliant, Grandpa!' I cried.

He shook his head sadly and his dandelion-clock hair flopped from side to side. 'Not really. The candle is burning the wax and that's using a sort of fuel. The smoke and the heat are still wasted. No, boy, it *still* isn't free power.'

'I could have told you that,' Susie said smugly as she blew out the candles, took the beans and tipped them into a saucepan. 'Stir this while I make some toast,' she ordered, bossy as ever.

'The problem is to get my powerless vehicle *started*. Something only *starts* to move if a *force* is used against it… otherwise it just sits there. It stays still because of a force called *inertia*. Once it starts it will keep going, and it only *stops* when another force is used. It keeps going through a force called *momentum*.'

'That's Newton's First Law of Motion,' Suzy said, very pleased with herself. She wasn't going to be pleased for much longer. But she didn't know that at the time.

I yawned. 'Who's this Newton?' I asked as the food was heating and Grandpa Grimlight got ready to go back to his experiments.

Susie looked at me with pity. She said nothing as she pulled a computer out of her school bag and punched a few keys. The name appeared on the screen…

NEWTON, Sir Isaac. 1642–1727.

English scientist and mathematician. In 1665 he thought up the famous three laws of motion. It is said that the idea came to him as he sat in his father's orchard. An apple fell from the tree and he began to wonder why everything fell to the ground.

'What did Newton say when the apple hit him on the head?' I asked Susie.

'I don't know.'

'He said "Caw!"' I laughed. Susie looked at me blankly. 'Apple...core...caw...geddit?'

'Yes, but I wish I hadn't,' said Susie sourly. She turned to Grandpa Grimlight. 'Want some beans, Grandpa?'

He took an egg from a carton beside the cooker. 'I always have a supply of hard-boiled eggs, so I can keep working and eat at the same time,' he explained and took one off to his room.

When I'd eaten Susie ordered, 'Now go and see if you can help Grandpa. You must have *some* sort of use. I'll print out this page on Newton for my homework file and find a few other facts about *Motion*.'

I wandered along the cobwebby corridors to Grandpa's workshop and found him dropping paper to the floor. Susie would have been furious and made me pick it up if I'd done that. 'What are you doing?' I asked.

He held out two pieces of paper. 'If I drop these two pieces of paper at the *same* time and from the *same* height then which one will hit the floor first?' he asked.

'Hah!' I cried. 'I know the answer to that one. They'll both hit the floor at the same time. Gravity pulls everything at the same speed. I did the test at home before I left.'

He nodded. 'And I say the one in my right hand will hit the floor first. Bet you a pint of ginger beer.'

'I bet you *two* pints!'

Grandpa Grimlight crumpled the paper in his right hand into a ball then let both pieces drop. The ball hit the ground first.

'That's cheating,' I grumbled.

'No that's the force of the air holding up the open sheet. It's what happens when you jump out of an aeroplane with a parachute. When I build my Powerless Bus then it will have to have *low* air resistance.'

'Like a streamlined car,' I nodded.

Somewhere in the house a clock struck eighteen. 'Ah! Six o'clock. Time for the news,' Grandpa Grimlight said and uncovered a television set from under a pile of books.

The news was shocking...

...AND THE DREADFUL DUCKPOOL DISAPPEARANCES DRAG ON DANGEROUSLY. TWO MORE PUPILS FROM DUCKPOOL PRIMARY WENT MISSING TODAY. ELVIS SMITH AND MYRTLE BRICK MET AT THE SWEET SHOP ON THE CORNER OF SHAVE CLOSE AND WERE LAST SEEN HEADING FOR THE DESERTED FAIRGROUND. MRS SMITH SOBBED, 'ELVIS WAS TOO SCARED TO GO TO SCHOOL SO HE SKIVED OFF INSTEAD'. MR BRICK WAS BEREFT. 'MY MYRTLE'S MISSING AND MOTION MAN'S THE MAIN SUSPECT!' HE MUTTERED MOURNFULLY.

MEANWHILE A DOZEN HARES HAVE ESCAPED FROM THE LOCAL ZOO. POLICE ARE COMBING THE AREA. AND POLICE HAVE ISSUED A DESCRIPTION OF TWO PEOPLE THEY WANT TO QUESTION IN CONNECTION WITH THE RUBY ROBBERIES. THESE TWO PEOPLE ARE JOINED AT THE HEAD BY A PAIR OF TIGHTS AND WERE LAST SEEN RUNNING FROM A CRASHED CAR...

I hurried out of the workshop, brushed past spiders and careered into the kitchen. 'Susie! Susie!' I cried. 'Myrtle and Elvis from Miss Trout's class... they're the latest victims. They've been...'

I stopped.

I was talking to an empty room.

Because *there* was my twin sister...

...gone!!!

Chapter 4

The kitchen door was open, the computer was glowing and the dishes weren't even washed. Susie *never* left dishes unwashed unless it was a real emergency – like when Boozle the dog got stuck in the cat flap.

I looked across the back garden that was as wild and tangled and terrifying as the front. The moon was rising behind the deserted fairground and the wooden frame of the huge roller coaster stood there like the skeleton of some giant dinosaur.

There was a flattened track in the grass and it led towards the fairground. Was *that* where Susie was headed?

I looked around for clues and glanced at the computer screen. Susie had typed in 'Search: motion'.

There, between 'motionless' and 'motion picture' was the answer. 'Motion Man', it said. And it explained what a motion man was.

'Where's the girl?' Grandpa Grimlight asked as he came into the kitchen munching a boiled egg.

'She's gone to the deserted fairground to rescue our friends,' I said. 'She's worked out that the kidnap victims are being taken there!'

'How do you know?'

I felt as clever as Sherlock Holmes. 'Elementary, My Dear Watson!' I cried.

Grandpa Grimlight walked over to the back door and looked at it closely. 'It's *black*!' he said.

I groaned. 'I said "el-e-ment-ary", not "lemon entry"!'

He turned a dial on his hearing aid and blinked as it whistled in his ear. 'What's that noise?' he asked.

With his hearing aid turned up his hearing was sharper than a bat's. I strained my ears and heard a faint creaking. Then I looked towards the skeleton roller coaster and saw a line of carriages creep creakily to the top of the highest peak. There wasn't a single person in the seats.

'Ah!' Grandpa Grimlight breathed. 'Watch the force of gravity send it round the track... a powerless train – my dream!'

The carriages rushed down the steep slope. It made me travel-sick just to look at it.

'I thought your dream was a powerless *bus*?'

'Same thing, stupid boy!' he snapped.

If he couldn't tell the difference between a bus and a train I wasn't going to argue.

I pointed to the computer screen. 'Look, Grandpa, the man who's kidnapping kids calls himself the Motion Man. And you said the owner of the fairground, Ebenezer Rugg, was a puppeteer. Well Susie's computer says that Motion Man is the old name for a puppeteer. So Ebenezer Rugg *is* the Motion Man. Susie's gone to investigate. And we have to go and help her.'

Grandpa nodded vaguely. 'Must investigate that powerless train,' he muttered. 'Could be the answer to the problems of the world.'

I began to pack Susie's bag with her computer and pushed in a couple of boxes of Grandpa's hard-boiled eggs. Then there was a rattle at the front door. I froze. I crept back along the cobwebbed corridor and saw something stuffed into the letterbox on the front door. It was a printed sheet. One of the spiders was reading it. I snatched it away from the hairy creature.

I took it to the kitchen table and smoothed it out. The faces of my friends Elvis and Myrtle stared back at me...

'I know that face,' Grandpa Grimlight said. 'I've seen it somewhere before.'

'Probably in the mirror,' I muttered.

'I *heard* that, boy. Just watch your manners or I won't take you *with* me.'

'Why? Where are you going?'

'To the old fairground.'

'To rescue Susie?'

'No. To see how that powerless roller coaster works.'

'So who's the man in the poster picture?' I asked.

'Ebenezer Rugg, of course!'

I grabbed Susie's bag and set off after Grandpa who was carrying his walking stick, a torch and a file marked, 'Powerless Bus – Top Secret'.

We stepped into the jungle he called a garden. The further we got from the house the darker it became. I tripped on a tangled plant and stumbled. Even Grandpa's voice had dropped to a loud whisper.

'Watch out for the creepers,' he said.

'What are creepers?'

'You'll find out when they creep up and get you,' he said then gave a vicious cackle. 'Heh! Heh! Heh!'

Have you ever seen pictures of dear, sweet, white-haired and caring grandparents? If you ever meet one then let me know. Because I haven't got one.

Even the light of the full moon didn't get through the undergrowth. At times we lost sight of the fairground. Finally we came to a high chainlink fence with a wire gate. A chain was wrapped around the handle and it was set in a heavy wooden frame. 'What we need here is a pulley,' Grandpa said.

'But…' I tried to argue.

Grandpa ignored me. 'What we need to do is simply lift

the gate off its hinges.'

'But…'

'Yes, I know it looks too heavy. But not when you use a little forces science.' In his hand he held a piece of paper torn from a book called *Science for Dunces*. I'd seen it before, we had that book in school! This page was all about *pulleys*…

LAZY LIFTING WITH POWERFUL PULLEYS (FOR DUNCES)

You Need:

① Coathanger-wire cut to about 20cm lengths (Get an adult to snip the wire because you're a dunce and will probably cut your finger off by mistake)

② Four cotton reels (Empty, of course you idiot)

③ String (Quite thick, but not so thick as you)

④ A pair of pliers to bend and cut the wire. (Do NOT use these to pinch your partner's bum or else)

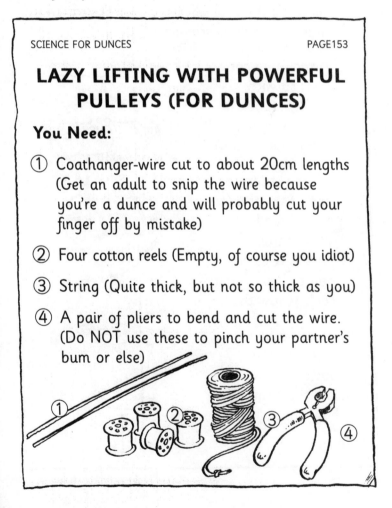

Making the Pulley:

1 Make the wires into triangles and hook one to the top of a door frame. (Triangles have three sides, by the way just in case you're rotten at maths as well as science)

2 Attach two cotton reels to each triangle (Look at the picture if you don't understand)

3 Tie the string to one of the triangles then thread the string through the pulleys (Get your dog to help if you can't follow this)

4 Attach a heavy object to the bottom triangle. Pull the string. See how easy it is?

PULL

Grandpa made himself busy with tools and wire while I peered through the wire. I'd given up trying to tell him that the chain around the handle was hanging loose. All we had to do was what Susie had done – open the gate and walk through.

After quarter of an hour he had fastened the pulley to the wooden frame and wrapped a rope around it. 'Now, boy, *pull*!'

I pulled. The gate groaned as the rusty hinges struggled to hold on to it. But after a minute the gate lifted off its hinges. I let go of the rope and it fell on to the gravel path inside the deserted fairground.

Grandpa Grimlight grinned – a horrible sight. 'Onward, boy! Onward and upwards! Through hardship to the stars… as the Royal Navy motto says!'

'I think it's the Royal Air Force that says that,' I said sadly. 'I don't think the navy spend a lot of time heading for the stars.' I followed him into the 'valley of death'… as a bunch of British soldiers said when they charged hopelessly at Russian cannon.

They didn't come back alive.

I didn't expect to either.

Chapter 5

Moonlight lit the concrete path as it twisted through the fair like a silver ribbon. Weeds pushed through the cracks and paper littered the ground. Then my brilliant brain clicked again.

A disused fairground wouldn't have fresh white paper on the ground. It would have been soaked to mush years ago. I stopped and picked up one of the sheets. I shone Grandpa Grimlight's torch on it and read...

Nightmare Park

OPENING SOON!

ON THE SITE OF THE OLD FAIRGROUND

FORGET MAGIC MOUSE LAND FOR MOUSEHEARTS!

THIS IS A THEME PARK FOR THE BRAVE-HEARTS!

INCREDIBLE POLLUTION-FREE POWERLESS RIDES!

TRULY TERRIFYING TRIPS!

CHAMBER OF HORRORS TO GIVE YOU
GOOSEBUMPS!

GHOST TRAIN TO
HAUNT YOUR DREAMS!

UNSUITABLE
FOR
PARENTS!!!

SEE LOCAL PRESS FOR DETAILS   PROPRIETOR: EBENEZER RUGG

39

'There you have half of the story,' I whispered. For some reason I wanted to keep our visit secret. 'Ebenezer Rugg, the Motion Man, plans to reopen the fair soon.' There was a soft swishing sound that grew into a roar as the roller coaster raced through the darkness. 'The moving carriages are just a test!'

'And the other half of the story is... what's happened to the kidnapped kids? What does Ebenezer Rugg want with them?' Grandpa Grimlight asked grimly.

I had a sudden horrifying vision. 'Your blue-toed wildcat!' I hissed hoarsely.

'Ah!' he sobbed, a little too loudly. 'Don't mention the blue-toed wildcat!'

'Sorry, Grandpa. But I was thinking of stuffed animals... have you ever seen *The Chamber of Horrors* in a waxworks?'

'No, but I've seen Granny Spark,' Grandpa said.

'Suppose you wanted a quick, cheap set of dummies for a waxworks. What would you do?'

'Kidnap some kids, stuff them and put them on display,' Grandpa nodded.

'Exactly!' I groaned.

'It may already be too late to save your sister what's-'er-name!' he muttered.

'I hope so,' I said, brightening up a little.

'What's that you say?'

'I said, "I hope *not!*"' I lied. Then I had a disturbing thought. 'I wonder if they still pay out the reward if we find the kids all stuffed?'

'Never mind that!' Grandpa said rubbing his hands like two sheets of sandpaper. 'If we find the secret of the powerless train we'll make a thousand times the reward money!'

'Really? And that roller coaster's the answer?' I asked.

'I don't know. Gravity takes it down the steep slope and momentum keeps it going round the track. The big question is what force takes it to the top of the steep slope in the first place?' Grandpa Grimlight said, walking forward towards the roller coaster.

'Electric motor?' I asked.

'There's no electric power to the fairground,' he told me. 'I saw the electricity men come and cut the power off six months ago.'

'A petrol motor?' I suggested.

'Can you hear one?' he asked.

I could hear a dog bark, an owl hoot and an ambulance siren in the distance. But the only sound from the fair itself was the creaking of a wheel and the soft beating of a drum. It was coming from a large wooden building that seemed to be trembling slightly.

I shone the torch on the sign above the doorway. It said '*House of Fun*' – but a piece of paper had been pasted over the last word and was flapping free. The paper had the word '*Fear*' written on it.

Someone had tried to change the *House of Fun* into the *House of Fear*. It needed someone fearless to investigate. Unfortunately there was no one else around so I had to do it myself... fearlessly.

I stepped into the darkened doorway. The floor was moving backwards and forwards under my feet. I gripped a hand rail to balance myself. Grandpa Grimlight followed.

We entered a room and the walls felt like ice. The rumbling sound and the beating of the drum was nearer now. Still, I decided to risk a quick shine of the torch. I flicked it on.

The sight that met me chilled my stomach like a look from Miss Trout. It was hideous, horrible and hair-raising. The boy that stared at me was twisted and leering and monstrous. He was shining a torch in my face. I held a hand across my mouth and he copied me in his cruel and twisted way. His torch began to shake and dance around and I realised that mine was doing the same. I caught sight of another boy, fat and round as a hamster. He was shining and shaking too. So was the boy with the waist of a wasp and the head of Frankenstein's monster to my left.

I took a step forward and they all stepped towards me. I was trapped!

I lowered my hand to scream but a rough hand smelling of hard-boiled egg wrapped itself around my face. 'Hush, boy!' Grandpa Grimlight hissed in my ear.

'It's only a hall of mirrors. You're looking at your own reflection all twisted and misshapen!'

I looked at the mirrors and three ugly boys stared back at me. 'Nnnng!' I tried to speak and struggled free. 'I know! I know! They never fooled me for a minute!'

I shone my torch on the gap between the mirrors that led out of the room. I caught sight of another of the posters. But this one had been turned around and someone had scribbled on the back. It was Susie's handwriting!

Simon

I think I've solved the mystery. Call the police. Tell them to watch out for the

And the last words disappeared in a squiggled line off the bottom of the paper. 'What does it mean, Grandpa?' I asked.

'It means we have to watch out for a squiggled line sliding off the end of a piece of paper!' he declared.

I could see he was going to be a problem. But he was getting excited and his parrot-beak nose was twitching excitedly. 'She has slid down a slope before she finished writing!' he told me.

'Yeah, Grandpa, everything slides down slopes. That's gravity.'

'No! You are wrong! You are forgetting about *friction*.'

'Like Enid Blyton or Roald Dahl?'

'No *friction*…not fiction. It's one of the things that's a problem with my Powerless Bus.' He rummaged in his secret file and came out with a magazine: *The Young Historian's Handbook*. He thumbed it till he came to a page marked 'Egyptian Engineers'.

'You're not a young historian, Grandpa. You're so old you could write history books from memory!' I muttered as I studied the page…

MOVING MOUNTAINS THE EGYPTIAN WAY

Ever wondered how the Ancient Egyptians moved those huge pyramid blocks across the desert when they didn't have wheels or cranes.

INSTEAD OF CRANES WE USED BRAINS!

Yes, those poor peasants had to drag those blocks across the sand and found it hard going.
Try this experiment:

You Need:

▲ An empty shoe box

▲ A piece of string

▲ Modelling clay

▲ Straws

WHAT YOU DO:

1. Attach the string to the box and put the modelling clay over the edge of the table. Put weight in the box till it doesn't move.

2. What's stopping it is the force of the table rubbing against the bottom of the box. Something we call 'friction'.

3. Put straws under the box and drop the modelling clay over the edge.

4. See how the box slides easily?

WE MOVED THESE STONES A PHARAOH WAY WITH THIS METHOD!

'Yeah, Grandpa, but what's this got to do with Susie's disappearance?'

'If you put something between the ground and the object you stop the friction!' he explained. 'Water on a road makes car tyres skid, ice under an ice-skater...'

'Jelly off a plate,' I said unhelpfully.

'Or polish on a floor!' Grandpa cried. 'This floor is highly polished! The friction's been reduced, you see?' he asked shining his torch down.

'No! Why would anyone want to do a thing like that?' I asked.

'It's a trap! When someone steps on it the floor tips and they'll slide off into the aaaaaaaaaaaaaaaaaaaaaaaa-aaaaaaaaaaaaaaaagh!'

Chapter 6

'I see what you mean, Grandpa!' I said as I watched him disappear into the candle-glow gloom below. Then I remembered Susie's science homework book, took it out of her bag and flipped through till I came to the 'Grip and Slip experiment'.

Grip and Slip

Science report by Susie Spark

Today our nice teacher Miss Trout gave us:

a wooden board   a pencil   a tape measure

and some squared paper

We took our shoes off. I was worried that my clean white socks would get dirty. Myrtle Brick's socks were too grubby to worry about. And as for the smell of Elvis Smith's feet it would make a dead cat in a sewer smell sweet. Anyway, we placed Myrtle's tap-dancing shoe on the board and tilted it until it began to slide.

We measured the height of the board - at least I did.

Then we placed my brightly polished black shoe on the board and tilted it till it slid, and we measured it again.

Lastly we put Elvis's trainer on the board. Quite honestly I'm surprised it didn't walk down the board by itself it was so disgusting.

We measured it, then we drew the result on a graph. Here it is.

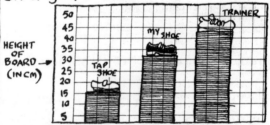

HEIGHT OF BOARD → (IN CM)

We discovered that Elvis's trainer had the most friction and stayed on longer, my leather soled shoe was next and Myrtle's tap dancing clog had hardly any grip. Next week we are going to repeat the experiment using different materials on the board — carpet, rubber mat, floor tile and polished wood. Elvis thinks we should try grass and some tarmac from the school yard, which is really quite clever for Elvis.

I looked down the tilted floor into the basement and called after Grandpa, 'Your shoes are more slippery than my trainers! I have more of that friction stuff. I won't slide down unless the board tips a little bit more-aaaaaaaaaaaaaaaaaaaaaaaaaaaaaaaaaaaaaaaaagh!'

The board tipped. I slipped.

I landed on Grandpa's head. At least it broke my fall. I don't know what he was grumbling about.

I looked around and a dozen pairs of eyes looked back. The eyes belonged to my schoolmates, the ones who'd been kidnapped! The room below the *House of Fear* was lit by candles. In the middle of the floor stood a wide wheel, just like the one Spike, our classroom hamster, has.

Inside the wheel about six of my mates were walking. As they walked the wheel turned and belts and pulleys and cogs turned. The other six were resting on low wooden beds on the floor. Slaves! Kept prisoner to drive the fairground rides!

Elvis was beating the drum to keep them marching in time. When he saw me he stopped. 'Simon!' he cried. 'Our hero! Come to rescue us!'

'You don't deserve it,' I told him. 'How did you get here?'

'We were promised free toffee apples, candy-floss and coconuts,' he sighed. Elvis held out a sheet of paper. It was one of Motion Man's posters. It read...

Do you want FREE SWEETS and CAKES?

DO YOU CRAVE CANDY CANES?

DO YOU DREAM OF DOUGHNUTS?

DO YOU LOVE LICKING LOLLIPOPS?

DO YOU HANKER AFTER HOT DOGS?

WANT TO FILL YOUR FACE WITH FAIRGROUND FOOD?

Then come along to the old fairground as soon as it gets dark each night. The loveable Motion Man will feed you full of his tastiest treats in exchange for a little work.

But **DON'T** tell your parents! You know how they hate you eating junk food that rots your teeth and gurgles in your guts. This is our little secret, kids. Just find the House of Fear and walk through.

Signed, your friend **The Motion Man**

'But we all fell into Motion Man's trap,' Myrtle explained. 'He appeared at that door,' she went on, nodding to a door at the top of some wooden steps.

A chubby girl called Gloria Gargle said angrily, 'He promised he'll give us the sweets when we've turned the wheel a thousand times. He says that will make all the machinery work tomorrow night when he opens 'Nightmare Park."

'He'll make enough money to pay his electric bill, and then he'll set us free,' Elvis said. 'All he's left us with is that thin porridge on the cooker.'

'Gruel?' I asked.

'Very cruel,' Elvis snivelled.

'How many turns have you managed?' Grandpa Grimlight asked.

'A hundred and seventy-seven,' Myrtle sniffed and wiped her nose on her sleeve. 'We're starving!'

Grandpa nodded. 'I was looking for the Powerless Train. But it's not powerless – it's powered by these children and they need feeding. Lucky you remembered to bring my box of hard-boiled eggs!'

'Hard-boiled eggs!' Gloria Gargle (the greedy grasping girl) grinned.

'Two boxes,' I said. 'Half a dozen in each.' I pulled them out of the bag and held them out.

'One egg each!' Gloria drooled and dribbled.

'No,' Grandpa said. 'There was a box of *cooked* eggs on the right of the cooker and a box of *raw* eggs on the other. You've mixed them up, boy. We could drop the raw eggs in the porridge and let them cook for five minutes.'

'But which are raw and which are cooked?' I asked.

'Crack one open to find out,' Gloria suggested.

'No. If we crack a raw egg then it'll be wasted and someone will have to go without,' Grandpa told her.

Gloria's fat face turned red with rage. 'How could you mix them up you...you...you *simple* Simon, you?'

She sounded just like Sister Susie. 'Here! Have you seen Susie Spark?' I asked.

'Only her legs. She slipped down the trap, just like you did,' Gloria explained. 'But she grabbed the frame and pulled herself out. She promised to come back and rescue us.'

Grandpa was looking around the room. 'All we need is a little science.'

'All I need is a hard-boiled egg,' Gloria said savagely and lunged at me. Grandpa stepped between us and pulled her fingers from around my throat.

'Wash a porridge bowl clean and I'll show you how to test if an egg is raw or cooked!' he ordered.

Gloria grudgingly left the eggs in my care and walked across to the stinking, slime-stained sink.

Suddenly there was a hammering on the door. 'Why has that drum stopped?' a voice bellowed. 'Why has the wheel stopped? Do I have to come in there and punish you?'

'That's the voice of Ebenezer Rugg,' Grandpa hissed.

'It's the Motion Man,' Myrtle squeaked.

I picked up the drum and thrust it at Elvis. 'Go on, Elvis. Beat it!'

'I can't,' he said.

'Why not?'

'Because the door's locked.'

I wanted to bite him on the ear. Instead I bit my knuckle. 'When I said *beat it* I didn't mean *beat it* I meant *beat it*! The drum, dummy.'

Elvis smiled. 'Why didn't you say so?' he said and began thumping on the drum. The children in the wheel began to march and the wheel turned.

Belts hissed, cogs clanked and axles creaked as the fair came to life again. The trap-door we'd fallen through was too high to reach. The door was locked.

I didn't like to tell Elvis that Grandpa Grimlight and I hadn't really rescued him. We'd simply joined the slaves.

Chapter 7

'Grandpa!' I hissed, close to his hearing aid. 'How are we going to get out?'

'Good question,' he nodded.

I waited. 'So? What's the answer?'

'We could telephone for help.'

'We haven't got a phone.'

'We could stop the wheel then wait for Ebenezer to open the door to investigate. We hide behind the door. When Ebenezer steps into the room we grab him and run out! I once saw Robin Hood do that in a film. It used to cost us sixpence to see those old black-and-white movies when we were kids.'

'I don't suppose Ebenezer Rugg saw the same films, did he?' I said.

'Of course.'

'Then he won't fall for it. Boozle the dog wouldn't fall for *that* old trick! Anyway the kids are too weak to jump on Spike the Hamster and capture him.'

'Once they've had an egg to give them strength they'll be fine. Otherwise we'll just have to wait for the police to work out where we've gone and come and rescue us,' I said.

Gloria was lurking and overheard us. 'Why aren't the police here already? They should be combing the town!'

'They are,' I said. 'For hares.'

'Combing their hairs?' she said angrily.

I didn't bother explaining. 'Maybe they're closer than we think,' I said. I pulled out Susie's pocket radio from her bag and turned it on to the local news programme...

...AND THE RUBY ROBBERS HAVE STRUCK AGAIN IN DUCKPOOL HIGH STREET. TWO PEOPLE WEARING A PAIR OF TIGHTS OVER THEIR HEADS STOPPED A LOCAL TEACHER, MISS TROUT, AND TOOK HER RING. AFTER PINCHING THE RUBY THEY HANDED BACK THE RING SAYING, "WE'RE ONLY AFTER RUBY, BOOBY!" THEN THEY RAN OFF. ANYONE WHO HAS SEEN TWO PEOPLE WITH THEIR HEADS IN ONE PAIR OF TIGHTS SHOULD CONTACT CHIEF INSPECTOR LETSBE AVENUE... SORRY, THAT SHOULD BE *LESLIE* AVENUE... CHIEF INSPECTOR AVENUE WAS ASKED TODAY WHAT HE'S GOING TO DO ABOUT THE RUBY ROBBERS.

"WE PLAN TO SET A SECRET TRAP. WE WILL PUT THE WORLD'S LARGEST RUBY ON DISPLAY IN THE JEWELLER'S SHOP IN DUCKPOOL HIGH STREET. UNKNOWN TO THE RUBY ROBBERS WE WILL HAVE POLICE SPIES WATCHING THE WINDOW TWENTY-FIVE HOURS A DAY. THEY WILL BE HIDDEN IN PILLAR-BOXES, CARS AND EVEN INSIDE LAMP-POSTS... IF WE CAN FIND FAT ENOUGH LAMP-POSTS OR THIN ENOUGH CONSTABLES. EVERY MAN, WOMAN AND OFFICER IN THE FORCE WILL BE SET TO CATCH THESE THIEVES."

'What about catching the Motion Man and setting us free!' I wailed.

... MEANWHILE POLICE WILL SCALE DOWN THE SEARCH FOR THE DISAPPEARING KIDS. A LETTER RECEIVED BY PARENTS SAID THE CHILDREN HAD ALL RUN OFF TO JOIN A LOCAL FAIR. IT ALSO SAID THEY WERE PERFECTLY HAPPY AND LIVING OFF CANDY FLOSS AND TOFFEE APPLES.

'I *wish*!' wailed Gloria. 'Not only do we have no toffee apples. We've no hope of being found by the police... and now we don't have any eggs.'

Grandpa Grimlight took the two boxes of eggs to the sink. He took an egg from each box and said to the six kids around him, 'It's a simple problem of *inertia*. Tell them what *inertia* is, Simon.'

It was worse than being in school. Everyone turned to look at me. 'Er. Inertia makes things stay still unless you use a force to move them.'

'A bit like Elvis Smith in class,' Myrtle Brick giggled.

'And momentum keeps things moving unless you use a force to stop them.'

'A bit like Gloria's spoon,' Myrtle went on happily, 'when you show her a plate of treacle pudding... ouch! Gloria, that really hurt!'

'See these gruel plates on the table?' Grandpa went on quickly as I untangled Gloria's fingers from Myrtle's hair. We looked at the disgusting mess in the bowls. 'They are staying on the table because of inertia!'

'They're staying on the table 'cos no one wants to eat the muck,' Gloria Gargle grumbled.

Grandpa Grimlight grabbed the paper tablecloth underneath the plates and gave it a sudden tug. Everyone gasped and waited for the crash of crockery that would bring Motion Man back. Amazingly the plates stayed on the table. '*Inertia* kept them there!'

(Baby Spark used to try this experiment at home... tugging at the tablecloth to get to its feet. It never worked for Baby Spark.)

Grandpa smiled and held the cloth proudly like some clever magician waiting for applause.

Instead he got a Gloria Gargle glare. 'This isn't getting me a hard-boiled egg!'

Grandpa took the clean bowl from Gloria and placed an egg in it...

EGG-STRA-ORDINARY INERTIA

Grandpa handed one box to Gloria. 'They're the raw eggs! Cook them for five minutes in the gruel pot and they'll be perfect!'

'Watch!' Gloria snapped at me.

'Why? What are you going to do?' I asked.

Her eyes were bulging in her head with anger. 'Simple Simon Spark, I will open your head and fill the empty space with this gruel if you do not hand me your *watch* right now.'

'My *watch*? You want my *watch*? Why didn't you say so?'

'I did,' she growled. 'Now can I have it?'

'Yes, Gloria, certainly Gloria.'

'Where is it?'

'On my bedside table in Grandpa Grimlight's house,' I told her.

'Nyaaaagggghhhh!' she screeched. 'I am NEVER going to get my egg at this rate! Doesn't anyone have a watch?'

No one answered.

'I've got one…but it doesn't have a second hand,' Grandpa sighed.

'Why not?' Gloria Gargle demanded.

'It was brand new when I got it… perhaps I should have bought it at a second-hand shop!'

Gloria stepped up to Grandpa and glared at him. 'You're the scientific genius around here. How do we count to five minutes without a watch?'

'I'm glad you asked me that,' Grandpa said.

  Gloria turned and looked at me. 'I knew he would be,' she sighed.

Chapter 8

'What we need is a pendulum,' Grandpa Grimlight said. 'Just a weight on a piece of string.' Grandpa took out his pocket watch and let it swing to and fro.

'Yeah!' Gloria Gargle said nastily. 'We could hang Simon Spark up by the feet from the frame of the machinery and let him swing from side to side!'

We could have tied a weight to the end of her long, greedy tongue and let *it* swing, but I was too polite to say so. (I was also scared of what she'd do to me if I said it.)

'How do we get the weight right?' I asked.

'Now it's a strange fact, but true, that the weight doesn't matter!' Grandpa Grimlight said. 'A pendulum will swing at the same speed no matter what weight you have on the end – a kilo of carrots or a carload of kangaroos. What changes the speed is the *length* of the string!'

'Brilliant!' I said. 'So what length of string makes it swing for exactly one second?' I asked.

'I can't remember,' Grandpa groaned while Gloria Gargle grimaced.

'I'll bet it's on Sister Susie's computer,' I said.

'If you tell me that's on your bedside table then I'll force feed this porridge into your left ear,' Gloria growled.

'It's in her schoolbag, which is right here,' I said smugly. There was enough battery power for the laptop computer to power up and I switched to the encyclopaedia.

I tapped in 'Pendulum' and the screen showed us what we needed to know…

The Know-it-all Computer Guide to...

PENDULUMS

Pendulums work because of Gravity.

Bet you didn't know… an Italian mathematician and scientist Galileo Galilei (1564–1642) was watching a chandelier swing in Pisa Cathedral one day. Groovy Galileo noticed it took the same time for it to complete the swing whether it was a long swing or a short swing. Try it!

Tie a bag of marbles to a piece of string and hang it from a hook. Let it go with long swings and see how long it takes to swing ten times. Then let it go for ten short swings. Same time!

Put more marbles in the bag. More weight but any swing, long medium or short, will always take the same time!

It's only when you shorten or lengthen the string that the speed changes.

'This isn't getting my egg cooked!' Gloria roared.

'Patience, girl,' Grandpa said and pressed *Page Down*.

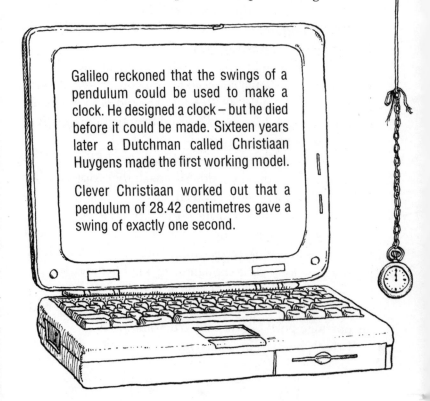

Galileo reckoned that the swings of a pendulum could be used to make a clock. He designed a clock – but he died before it could be made. Sixteen years later a Dutchman called Christiaan Huygens made the first working model.

Clever Christiaan worked out that a pendulum of 28.42 centimetres gave a swing of exactly one second.

'Hooray!' Gloria cried. 'Now we just measure a pendulum of 28.42 centimetres and count while it swings five minutes... that's five times sixty... that's... er...'

'Thirty thousand?' I guessed.

'Thirty thousand!' Gloria cried. 'Me stomach will think me throat's been cut if it has to wait that long.'

'It's three hundred,' Grandpa Grimlight said as he took Susie's ruler from her pencil case and measured a piece of string. He tied his pocket watch to the end and fastened the string to a wooden beam. 'The young lad with the drum can count while he beats.'

'Elvis! Count to three hundred,' I ordered.

'Three hundred?' he said confused. 'How can I do that? I've only got ten fingers.'

Grandpa sighed. 'You six who aren't in the wheel... stand in a circle. Each count to ten on your fingers in turn. Every circuit is a minute. Ready?' The old man organised us, set the pendulum swinging and dropped the eggs into the bubbling gloop of gruel.

'What we really need are some soldiers,' Elvis said.

'Yeah! Shoot the door down, smash that Motion Man feller and escape,' Gloria agreed.

'No,' Elvis dribbled. 'I meant to dip in me egg.'

At last they were ready. The kids had a choice of cold or hot eggs and took turns eating and treading the wheel. Finally they looked fit enough to tackle Ebenezer Rugg.

'Now,' Grandpa said. 'I have a plan.'

'Hide behind the door and bash the Motion Man with his porridge pot!' Gloria said gruesomely.

'I think he may be ready for that,' I said. 'The Lone

Stranger did that in episode 17 of *Rattlesnake Road Robbers*.'

'Not to mention episodes 3, 6, 8, 11, 12 and 15,' Grandpa agreed. 'No, my plan is to get him all the way into the middle of this cellar. I will then show him something interesting in the middle of this table. While he bends over to look...'

'I'll smash his conk with the porridge pot!' Gloria offered.

Grandpa Grimlight shook his head wearily. 'No, girl. You will quietly slip out of the door and run into Duckpool town.'

'Well, that's a great plan,' Gloria sneered. 'You're a senile turkey-brain!'

'That's an insult!' I objected.

She turned on me. 'Sorry. It is. It's an insult to *turkeys*.' She turned back on Grandpa Grimlight. 'My friends have been tramping round that wheel for hours – some have been here for days... they haven't any strength left. They *can't* run!'

'My nose has been running all day,' Myrtle Brick sniffed. Gloria ignored her.

Grandpa looked at the round-faced, red-faced girl and said, 'You are quite right. I have another plan for you once you get out of here.' He bent his head close to hers and whispered. Then he handed her the pulley he'd used to lift the fairground gate.

Gloria grinned. It wasn't a pretty sight. 'You're not as stupid as you look,' she said. 'How will we find the police?'

'They're on a stake-out of the jeweller's shop in the High Street,' I said and flicked on the radio...

x

67

...AND HERE IS THE MIDNIGHT NEWS. IN THE TRAP TO CATCH THE RUBY ROBBERS THE POLICE HAVE DUCKPOOL HIGH STREET UNDER THE EYES OF TWENTY-FIVE POLICE OFFICERS. THERE WOULD HAVE BEEN TWENTY-SIX BUT ONE OFFICER DISGUISED AS A TREE HAD A NASTY ACCIDENT WITH A PASSING DOG. HE HAS GONE BACK TO THE STATION TO CHANGE HIS TROUSERS. IT WOULD HAVE BEEN WORSE FOR THE OTHER TREE OFFICERS, ALL FROM SPECIAL BRANCH, BUT THE DOG SET OFF IN PURSUIT OF AN ESCAPING CHAIR... SORRY, I'LL READ THAT AGAIN... THE DOG SET OFF IN PURSUIT OF AN ESCAPING *HARE*.

'A High Street full of police. Perfect,' Gloria chuckled. 'What about the plan to keep Motion Man busy?' she asked.

Grandpa nodded. He burrowed into Susie's school bag and came up with scissors and card and glue and began to make a model. Five minutes later he ordered, 'Stop beating the drum, boy! We are ready for Ebenezer Rugg!'

Chapter 9

The beating stopped. The only sound in the cellar was the plopping of porridge on a gas ring, the sputtering of candles and the ticking of Grandpa Grimlight's watch.

Then there was the faint sound of footsteps approaching the door. *Two* pairs of footsteps! All eyes turned to the door at the top of the stairs. A key rattled in the lock. The door opened. Ebenezer Rugg stood there – the Motion Man.

He was slightly balder than an egg but the same shape. The only hair on his pale face were the enormous eyebrows that arched up like caterpillars. His bulky body blocked the door. He stepped forward and a head appeared from behind him. It was Susie!

'Hi, kids! I've arrested this monstrous Motion Man and come to set you free.'

'Susie!' Gloria cried. 'How did you do it?'

'Just took Grandpa Grimlight's wartime revolver and

stuck it in this putrid puppeteer's back.'

'Pull the trigger! Pull the trigger!' Gloria Gargle urged.

Susie pushed Ebenezer Rugg in the back and said, 'March.'

The miserable Motion Man walked down the steps towards us. Every step left the way to freedom nearer. Just three more steps... two... one... then...

'Hey! That's clever, Susie!' Elvis Smith cried. 'You haven't got a gun at all. You just poked him in the back with your finger and pretended! Just like the Lone Stranger in *Gunfight at the OK Canal*!'

Everyone groaned. Ebenezer Rugg turned and stared at Susie. My sister lowered her finger.

Then Rugg roared. 'Back to work you uncouth kids! I only have the Ghost Train left to test then I'm ready to open Nightmare Park!'

Grandpa stepped forward into the candlelight. 'Amazing! It's my old friend, Ebenezer Rugg, isn't it? We were boys together – at least I was. You were the brightest lad in Duckpool Secondary Modern School... and my very best friend!'

Rugg peered into the gloom. He took the final step off the stairway and into the room. The way was clear behind him for the kids to escape. No one moved.

'Gordon?' he said. 'Gordon Grimlight? Is that you? After all these years?'

Grandpa stepped forward and held out his arms. He clasped the fat puppeteer to his chest. Susie on the top step began to signal the kids to tiptoe over to the stairway. But I was standing beside Grandpa and couldn't get past without making Ebenezer Rugg suspicious. I had to be a hero. I had to stay while my schoolmates escaped.

'How have you been, Ebenezer, old pal? What have you been up to?'

Six kids were wearily climbing the creaking stairs.

'I've been inventing the powerless fairground!' the bald man boasted.

Two more slipped up the stairs. Four to go.

'Wind power?' Grandpa asked as if he were interested.

'No use on a calm day,' Rugg shrugged. 'I've been using child power.'

Two more kids crept through the door. Only Gloria Gargle and Elvis Smith to go.

'See what I have here, then!' Grandpa Grimlight said and he pointed to the model on the table. 'The real answer you've been searching for! Gravity power!'

I've tried to draw Grandpa's model as clearly as I can remember. Here's the sketch I did when I got home...

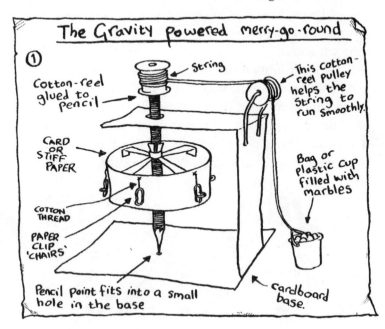

The Gravity powered merry-go-round

① Cotton-reel glued to pencil → String

This cotton-reel pulley helps the string to run smoothly.

CARD OR STIFF PAPER

Bag or plastic cup filled with marbles

COTTON THREAD

PAPER CLIP 'CHAIRS'

Pencil point fits into a small hole in the base

cardboard base.

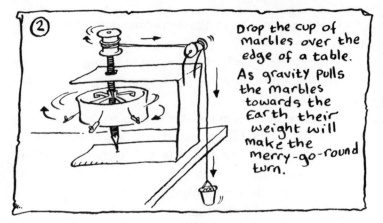

Drop the cup of marbles over the edge of a table.

As gravity pulls the marbles towards the Earth their weight will make the merry-go-round turn.

Grandpa let go of the weight and the merry-go-round began to spin. 'Wonderful!' Rugg raved. 'The powerless fairground is in my grasp!' The paper-clip chairs flew out... and so did Gloria and Elvis.

Susie signalled for me to follow. I slid past the marvelling Motion Man and joined my sister. 'Well done, Susie.'

She looked pleased. 'How will we get Grandpa out?' she whispered.

'He'll get himself out, don't worry,' I said.

At that moment he was saying to Rugg, 'My invention is all yours, my dear, dear old friend!'

The caterpillar eyebrows drew together and he frowned. 'Hang on, Grimlight. I've just remembered... we *weren't* friends at school. We were deadly *enemies*! We

hated each other. You cheated me out of my toy bus, I remember now.'

'I always liked buses,' Grandpa said as he backed towards the stairs.

'You threw a coin and said, "Heads it's mine and tails it's not yours" – you cheated me! And you're cheating me now with this model.'

'It *works*,' Grandpa said, setting his foot on the first step. The weight had reached the bottom of the string and the merry-go-round had stopped.

'No it doesn't. You need *some* sort of *power* to raise the weight back to the top again. It isn't powerless at all. You cheat, Grimlight!' The fat man took a rolling step towards Grandpa, his podgy fists stretched in front of him. 'Well, cheats never beats!'

Grandpa clattered up the steps, Susie and I ran through the door and closed it after him. The key was still in the lock and she turned it smartly as the massive body hit the other side and the Motion Man roared with pain and anger.

'Run!' Grandpa cried.

'Where to?'

'To our getaway vehicle,' he panted.

'What's that?' I gasped.

'The Ghost Train, boy, the Ghost Train!'

Chapter 10

No sooner had Susie locked the door than a fat fist smashed through. Before she could take the key out of the lock the Motion Man's hand was groping for it.

'Run!' Susie cried. We ran. We ran through the dark and deserted fairground.

Past the waiting waltzers. Past the dingy dodgems and the rickety rollercoaster. Past the gallopers on the roundabouts, their gold manes shining a ghastly green in the moonlight. Past the silent swings and the shuttered stalls till we reached the Ghost Train.

Gloria had everyone in their seats, metal bars clamped across their laps to hold them steady. 'Push, Simon! Push Susie! You're the strongest,' she ordered as Grandpa fastened himself into the cab of the locomotive. It had, 'Harry the Happy Engine' on its side and a stupid grinning face painted on its front.

'We'll go around in circles!' I argued. I stood behind the last carriage and pushed towards the bat-black tunnel. 'This inertia's killing me!' I panted as I struggled to get the train moving. But once they were rolling it became easier.

We rattled past coffins and skeletons and ugly devils, clunked through doors and swished through trailing creepers. 'Jump aboard!' Gloria shouted. We climbed into the last carriage and pulled the safety bar across our laps.

The Ghost Train's last horror was the most gruesome of all. It roared and leapt at us crying, 'You cheated me!'

It was Ebenezer Rugg. He grasped the last carriage and tried to haul us back but was dragged along. 'The momentum's too great!' I cried happily.

'You'll stop sooner or later,' he snarled and jumped on the tail to wait.

'Hold tight!' Gloria cried. 'This is where we lifted the track!'

The train bumped and jumped. Instead of swinging around the corner and back to the start of the circuit it headed straight for the wooden wall. There was a splintering crash as we broke through and a gush of cool night air smacked us in the face.

After the darkness of the tunnel we could see the moon and stars above and the orange and blue lights of Duckpool in the valley below us. 'Gravity!' Grandpa roared happily as we headed down the hill and built up speed.

'How do we stop when we get to the bottom?' Susie cried.

'Friction,' Grandpa called back from his seat in the cab. 'Stick your feet out of the doors.'

The night dew was thick on the grass and our feet just skidded. The Ghost Train went faster and faster. I wondered if Harry the Happy Engine was still smiling. Now we could make out the shops in the High Street below us.

I looked for Susie's computer to give us a clue but I'd left it in the cellar of the *House of Fear*. Instead I came across a book called *Have Fun with your Teddy*.

'What's this?' I gasped as the wind snatched at my breath and tore it out of my mouth.

'The answer!' Susie cried and opened it.

Make a Parachute

Do you want to watch your teddy jump off your roof? Then why not make him this jolly little parachute?

You need:

A plastic carrier bag, six pieces of string, some scissors – and a helpful mummy or daddy to do all that nasty dangerous cutting for baby poo. (And to read these rather complex instructions to a pre-school, non-reading rug-rat like you!)

To make it:

1. Cut a large circle from a plastic carrier bag

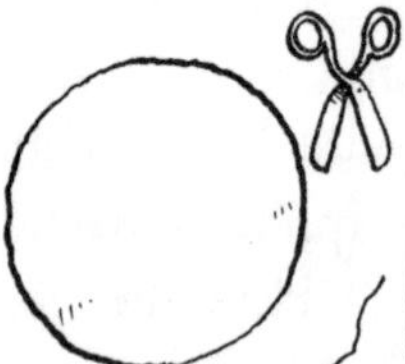

2. Tape each string around the edge of the circle

3. Tie the loose ends to Teddy

4. Throw Teddy off the highest tower you can find and watch him float safely to the ground.

Wasn't that fun? Bet you're glad it wasn't you on the end of that parachute, eh, baby poo? Well it will be next time if you don't go to sleep without crying.

Fun Fact:

Did you know, full-sized parachutes have a hole in the top otherwise the parachutist would have a rough ride. The first parachutist, Andre-Jacques Garnerin, in 1797 didn't know this. He was airsick from the bumpy ride – he threw up all over the people waiting below! And in 1912 an Austrian Franz Reichalt invented a new parachute. "I am confident of success!" he announced before he jumped off the top of the Eiffel Tower. The parachute failed. Franz was scraped off the pavement. So the message is... leave the parachuting to dear old Teddy!

'Right!' Susie cried. 'Everyone take off their coats and hold them out to catch the air.'

'I thought the radio said the police had caught all the hares,' Elvis argued.

'Air, not hare. Now shut up, Elvis, and do it!' Gloria shouted.

But it was too late to slow us much. We were at the back of the shops and heading for a narrow lane between the butcher's and the newsagent.

We shot through the lane and out into the High Street. The jeweller's shop glowed golden ahead of us and a huge red jewel glinted in the window.

'We're going to hit that window!' Susie cried. 'Hold on to your safety bars!'

'No! There's a tree in the way,' Grandpa Grimlight called and rang the bell on the cab of the engine.

The tree heard the bell, turned, screamed and dived out of our way. As we raced past I'll swear he cried, 'It's a nightmare for elm trees!'

The front buffers of the train hit the low wall under the jeweller's window and we came to a sudden stop. But Ebenezer Rugg had been standing at the back of the train. When the train stopped he kept moving, up and over our heads.

'Momentum, you see?' Susie said happily. 'That's why you should always wear a seat belt.'

Ebenezer Rugg shot towards the window of the jeweller's shop. His bullet head broke the glass and he ended clutching the large red jewel. In ten ticks of Grandpa's pendulum he was buried under a mass of blue uniforms, red

pillar boxes, green trees all waving handcuffs and blowing whistles. Two large police dogs sniffed at the trees and began to lift their legs just to add to the confusion.

At last Ebenezer Rugg was led away, still dazed, to a waiting police van. An inspector with silver buttons glistening walked over to Grandpa. 'I am Chief Inspector Leslie Avenue. Well done, sir, you have helped us to capture that dangerous criminal.'

'Yeah, Grandpa,' I said. 'You've nabbed the Motion Man! That's ten thousand pounds reward!'

'No, no, no!' the Inspector said. 'He was the Ruby Robber. That's ten thousand pounds reward.'

Susie stepped forward quickly. 'He was the Motion Man *as well* as the Ruby Robber... Grandpa Grimlight gets *twenty* thousand pounds.'

'Twenty thousand it is,' the policeman nodded. 'I have it here in a carrier bag,' he offered, and sent Grandpa Grimlight home with an escort of a lamp-post and a pillar box.

The last we saw of Grandpa he was crying, 'I'll be able to build a new laboratory *and* get my grass cut now!'

'Another Spark File successfully closed,' I said to Sister Susie.

'Not quite,' she said. 'I like things to be really tidy. You know that.'

'I know that.'

I followed Susie over to two people cleverly disguised as police constables. 'Hand over Miss Trout's ruby,' Susie demanded. 'The game is up. You are the *real* Ruby Robbers and I will tell the real police if you don't hand over our teacher's jewel.'

The constable in a skirt handed over a fistful of rubies. 'How did you know?' the young robber sighed.

'Because there were supposed to be twenty-five police here in the trap but I counted twenty-seven. Two had to be fakes.'

'Yeah,' the man said, 'But how did you know it was *us* that were the fakes?'

Susie wasn't pleased that I stole her glory. But I *had* to say it. 'The pair of tights you have over your head was the giveaway.'

Two heads in one pair of tights nodded, sadder and wiser.

'You're a great detective, Susie,' I said. 'You should join the force.'

'I think we've had quite enough of forces for one day, Simon. Time we went home.'

I was forced to agree.

Here is a list of experiments in this book. Have you tried them all?

✳ Science Notes ✳

GRAVITY
DEMONSTRATION
50p

✦Science Notes✦

GRAVITY
DEMONSTRATION
50p

Science Notes

✦ Science Notes ✦

✳ Science Notes ✳